WEIRDO 3
EXTRA WEIRD!

Scholastic Press
345 Pacific Highway Lindfield NSW 2070
An imprint of Scholastic Australia Pty Limited (ABN 11 000 614 577)
PO Box 579 Gosford NSW 2250
www.scholastic.com.au

Part of the Scholastic Group
Sydney • Auckland • New York • Toronto • London • Mexico City • New Delhi • Hong Kong • Buenos Aires • Puerto Rico

First published by Scholastic Australia in 2014.

National Library of Australia Cataloguing-in-Publication entry
Author: Do, Anh, author.
Title: WeirDo 3, extra weird / written by Anh Do; illustrations by Jules Faber.
ISBN: 9781743627051 (paperback)
Series: Do, Anh. WeirDo; 3.
Target Audience: For primary school age.
Other Authors/Contributors: Faber, Jules, 1971-, illustrator.
Dewey Number: A823.4

Typeset in Grenadine MVB, Push Ups and Lunch Box.

Printed by RR Donnelley.
Scholastic Australia's policy, in association with RR Donnelley, is to use papers that are renewable and made efficiently from wood grown in responsibly managed forests, so as to minimise its environmental footprint.

28 27 26 25 24 22 23 24 / 2

ANH DO

Illustrated by JULES FABER

WEIRDO 3

EXTRA WEIRD!

A SCHOLASTIC PRESS BOOK
FROM SCHOLASTIC AUSTRALIA

SQUAWK!

CHAPTER 1

This is my mum.
She looks normal,
but
she's
not.

This is Mum after she's fallen in the bin at the park.

She falls in all the time when she's picking up empty cans.

If she fills up a big bag, she gets a dollar from the can company.

A **whole** dollar!

I told you she was **cheap**!

When we were little, Mum even told us that the **ice-cream truck** only plays his **music** when he's **run out** of ice-cream!

Sometimes Mum finds **other things** in the park bins, too.

My dad and my granddad are **even weirder** than my mum.

I was watching them **fooling around** on the monkey bars when I heard a **scream!**

It was my sister, Sally!

EEEK!

SPIDER!

Lately Roger's been picking up and eating things he really shouldn't.

Like gum from my shoe.

Worms from the backyard.

And an **old chip** that had been under the couch since **dinosaur times**.

Sally's **scared** of spiders, but **I'm not**.

'Watch this!' I said.

Then I jumped up

and landed hard

on the other side of the

see-saw.

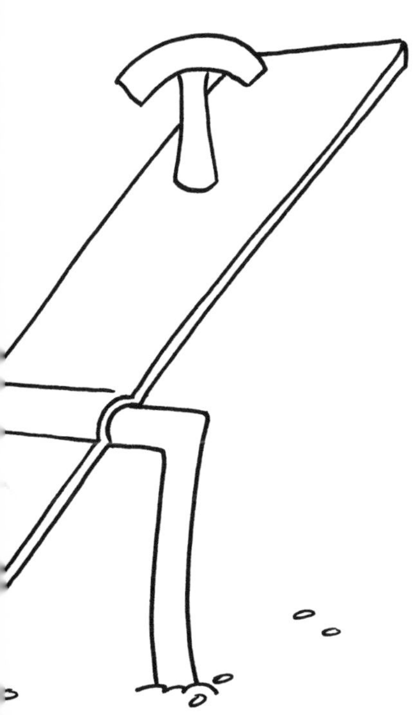

The spider went flying!

WHEEEEEEEEE

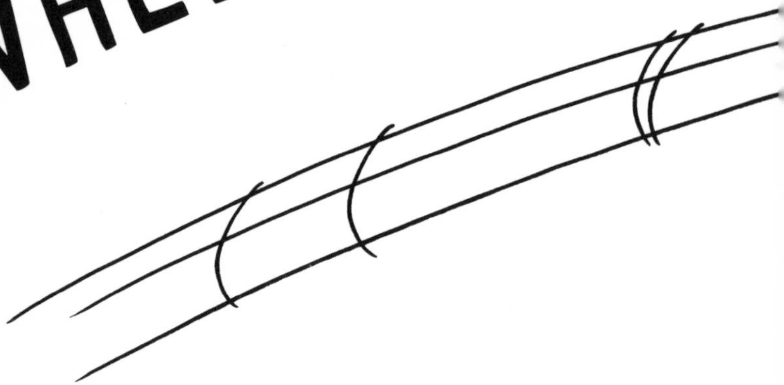

EEEEEEE!

'Thanks,' said Sally. 'That was close!'

But then all of a sudden something

WAY

WAY

WAY

WORSE

flew in my face!

LADYBUG!!!

I ran for my life!

I ran past Dad and Granddad on the monkey bars.

I ran past some kids playing soccer. ››››

I ran the fastest I'd ever run before! ❯❯❯❯

Phew! That was close!

So maybe I haven't told you yet . . .
but I'm **TERRIFIED** of ladybugs.

Some people are scared of

spiders,

or ghosts,

or great white sharks...

but nothing scares me more than those red and black little spotty

monsters!

Why? I don't know... Maybe because

I'M EXTRA WEIRD!

My name is WEIRDO. First name Weir, last name Do (yep, rhymes with go).

I guess with a name like that I was always going to be a bit strange!

Roger is my little brother, and he isn't afraid of ladybugs. In fact, Roger isn't afraid of **anything**!

'Weir, come back!' Sally called out. 'The ladybug's gone.'

'Okaaaaaay,' I said.

I **love** the swings. I love swinging next to Sally so we can see who can go the **highest**.

Granddad gave us a push to get us started.

I went **really high** . . . but Sally went **higher**.

So I went **higher again**.

And then Sally went **even higher than that**!

But just when I thought Sally had won, something **whacked** me on the **bottom** and gave me an **enormous push**!

I went **flying**!

I swung **SO HIGH** . . .

that I went the

whole way around!

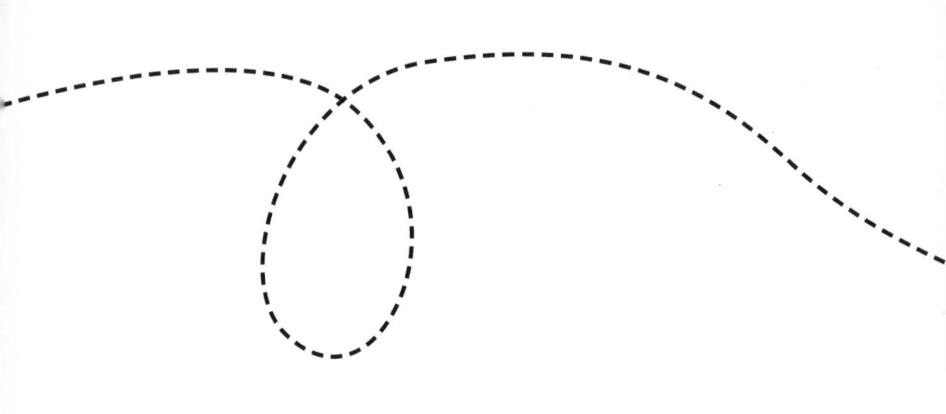

WOW!

WHOAAA!

Then I heard **Blake Green** call out.

I went to kick the soccer ball to him . . .
but I **completely missed** and **landed**

OOOF!

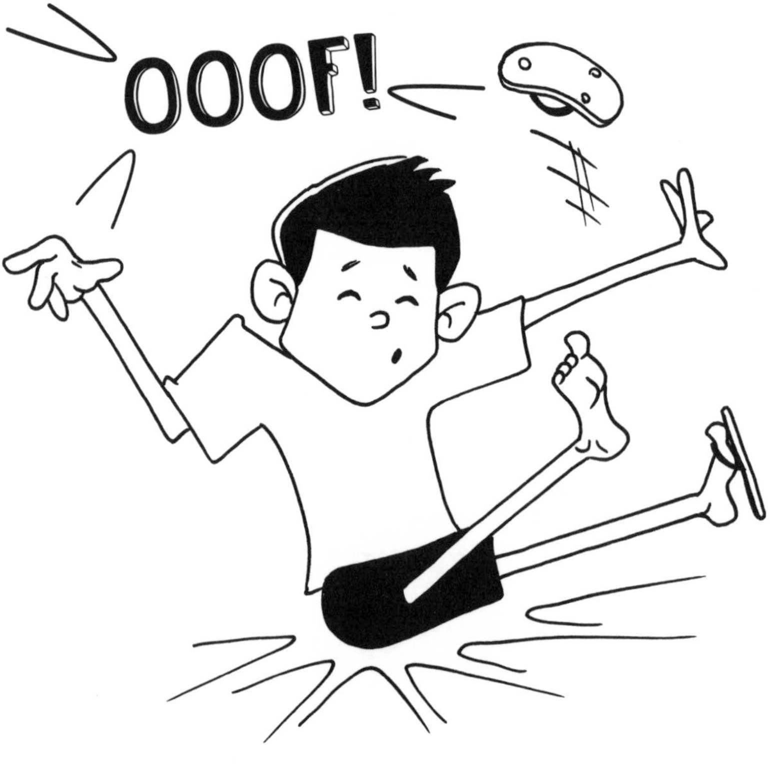

I stood up and tried to kick the ball again.

But instead of sending it **flying over** to where Blake and his friends were waiting, the ball went **right up** ...

into a tree

and nearly hit a bird!

The bird got such a fright . . .

SQUAWK!

SPLAT!

OOOPS!

. . . it **pooped** on me!

YUUUKKKKK!

BIRDIE POOP!

I **picked up** the ball this time and **ran** all the way over to Blake and his friends.

'Here you go,' I said, handing it to them.

NO PROBLEM AT ALL!

23
CLOWNS!

CHAPTER 2

Mum is **always** on the lookout for **weird contests to enter**.

That's because my family has **weird skills** that are only useful for winning stuff in **weird contests**.

Like Mum is **great** at guessing how many things **fit** into other things . . .

Last year, she entered a **jellybean guessing competition**...

We won! Yay!

Roger ate all 367 in one afternoon.

When Granddad's robotic ear is working, he has super-dooper hearing.

One time, Granddad guessed the **secret sound** on the radio . . .

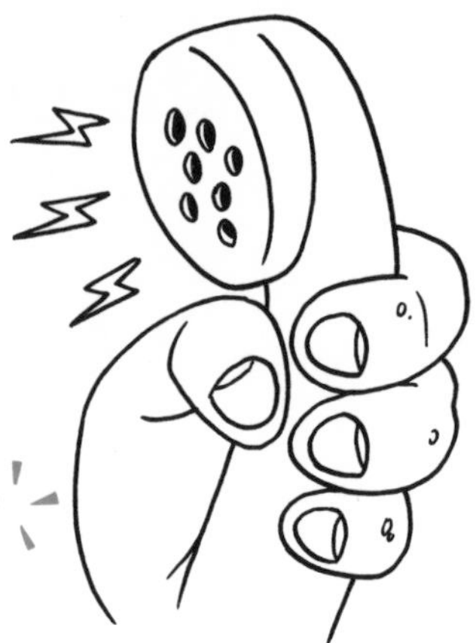

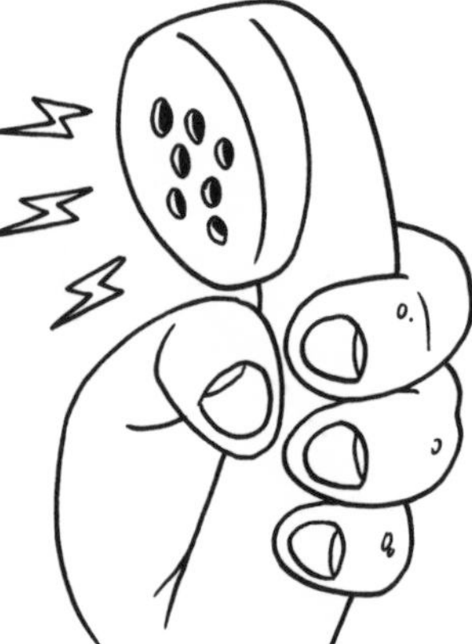

ITCHY BOTTOM SQUIRREL!
ITCHY BOTTOM SQUIRREL!

We won **five hundred dollars** and we bought Granddad a **new** set of **teeth**! His old ones were falling apart!

old teeth

new teeth

old teeth

Sally's **really good** at **hoopla**.

When she grows up

she could get a job as a **rhino catcher** for the **zoo**.

Now Mum has entered Dad into a *Talent Quest* **at the mall**. The prize?

Not **money**.

Not **jellybeans**.

Not even **teddy bears**!

The prize:

A year's supply of DOG FOOD!

'But we don't even have a dog!' I said to Mum.

My mum says **'Just in case!'** a lot. It's true, in our garage we have a **camel's saddle**, **just in case** we ever buy a camel.

We also have an **anchor**, **just in case** we ever buy a ship.

We even have some **jeans** that are **eight sizes too big**, **just in case** Dad starts eating too much.

Dad's going to **dance** at the *Talent Quest* so he's been practising **a lot**!

You might remember some of his **cool** moves.

robot dance

still the
worm dance

He's added some **new** ones, too!

the sprinkler
changing-
the-
lightbulbs
the snake

All of us are helping him.

Granddad showed him how to do the **itchy bottom squirrel**.

Mum showed him the **pick up empty cans**.

Roger showed him the **jellybean tummy ache**.

Sally showed him
the rhino-catching
cowboy.
Even Blockhead
helped out with the
wanna-fight?
WANNA
FIGHT?

I showed Dad one, too. I called it the **ladybug shake.**

Next I showed him the **killer whale.**

Dad **loved** them all!

'Do you think I'm in with a chance?' he asked us.

'For sure!' we all said.

'Woof woof!' said Blockhead, our bird.

'Farter!' said Roger. **'Farter! Farter!'**

That's right, every time Roger tries to say 'father', it still comes out sounding like **'Farter'**!

Dad does fart **a lot**. If he can dance as well as he farts,

that

DOG FOOD

is ours!

SNOT
FUNNY!

CHAPTER 3

Today Henry brought his **soccer ball** to school so that we could **practise** for the soccer **try-outs**.

It turned out **a lot** of people wanted to make the team! Bella, Clare, Wendy and even Toby 'the moneybox' Hogan wanted to practise with us.

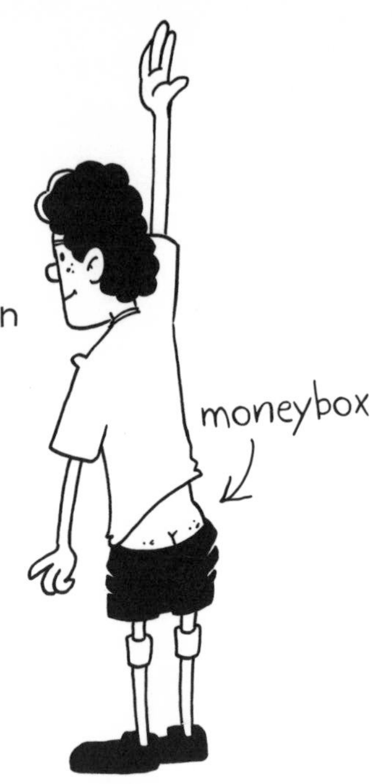

Henry passed the ball to Clare, and Clare passed the ball to me.

I had to pass it to Bella, so I **really** didn't want to **mess** it up.

I kicked the ball **MUCH harder** than I needed to. The ball flew **way past** Bella …

It went right through the **staff room window** …

NOOOOO

OOOOOOOOOOO!

and knocked over
three bowls of noodles ...

SPLOSH! SPLASH!

splashing three cranky teachers.

NOT AGAIN . . .

So that's why I ended up in afternoon **detention**!

I sat down next to **James Nott** at the back of the room. When you say his name fast, it sounds like **James Snot**.

Which is actually a good way to describe him, cos he's one of those people who **always** has a **runny nose**!

WANT A TISSUE?
WHAT FOR?

Plus he's one of those kids who **never** **laughs at anything**, even when

everyone else

is

LAUGHING SO hard

they're on the

floor!

And he always goes, 'It's not funny.'
Which

ALWAYS

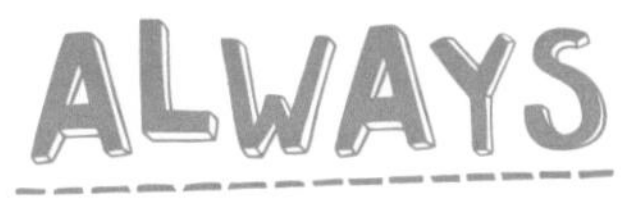

sounds

more

like . . .

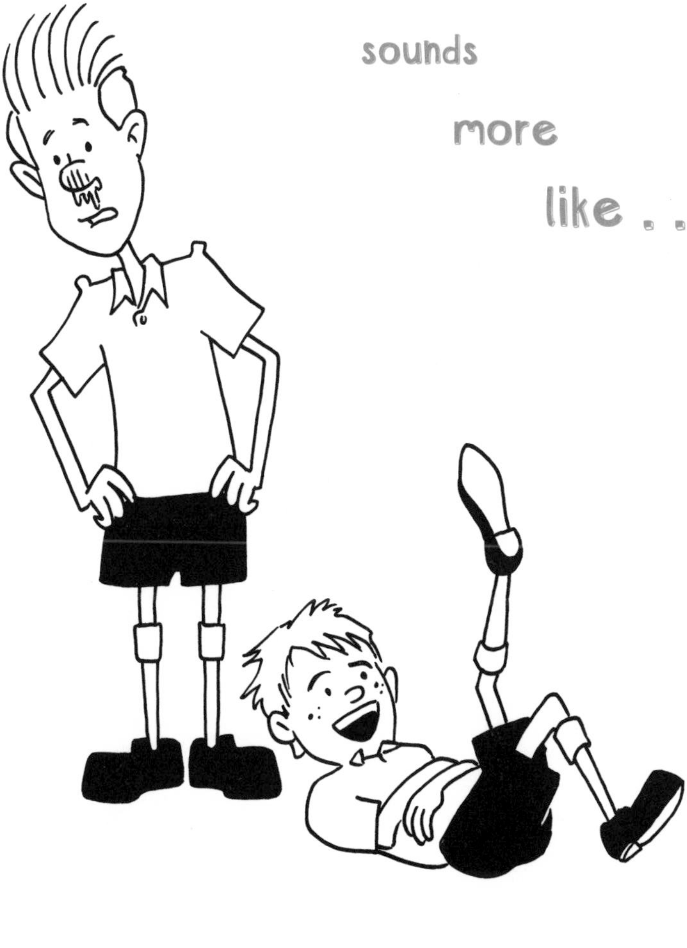

snot FUNNY

If only he could **earn money** making **snot**. If he could sell **snot-in-a-pot** as craft glue, he'd be a **billionaire**!

'What are you doing?' I asked him.

'Writing.'

'Writing what?'

'A book about boogers,' he replied.

‘Yep. There are so many kinds . . .

Crusty ones that are like little nose rocks.

Sticky ones that stick to your finger . . .

You try to flick it off, but then it just sticks to your other finger . . .

The **best boogers** are the **s t r e t c h y** ones that come out like a **long green noodle**.'

HA!

I liked the booger book!

HOW ABOUT THOSE SHY ONES THAT HIDE RIGHT UP THE BACK AND YOU JUST CAN'T REACH THEM?

'Back to work, boys,' said the teacher.

Since James showed me his snot drawings, I decided to draw him some mixed-up animals.

First I drew a **dolphin** ...

It looks cute ... until you cross it with a **ladybug**!

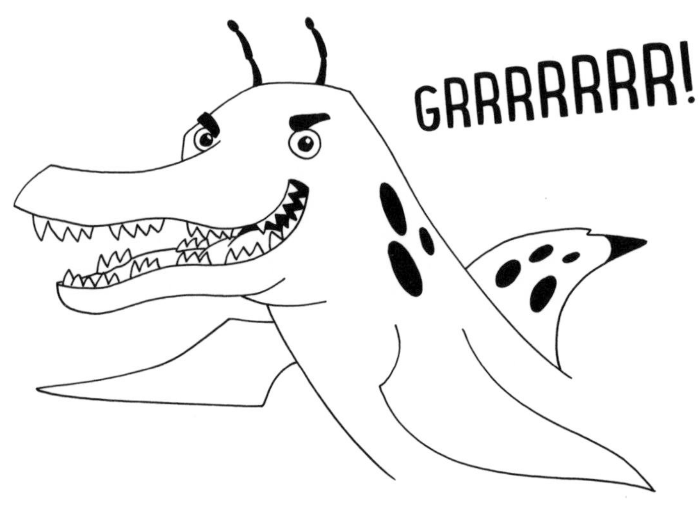

Then I drew a **teddy bear** ...

That looks okay too . . . until you cross it with a **ladybug**!

Next I drew a **great white shark** ...

Sharks are **scary**, but they become **even scarier** when you cross them with a **ladybug**!

RAAAAAAAAAAH!

Then I drew a picture I didn't show James . . .

A

B Fold line B over to meet line A

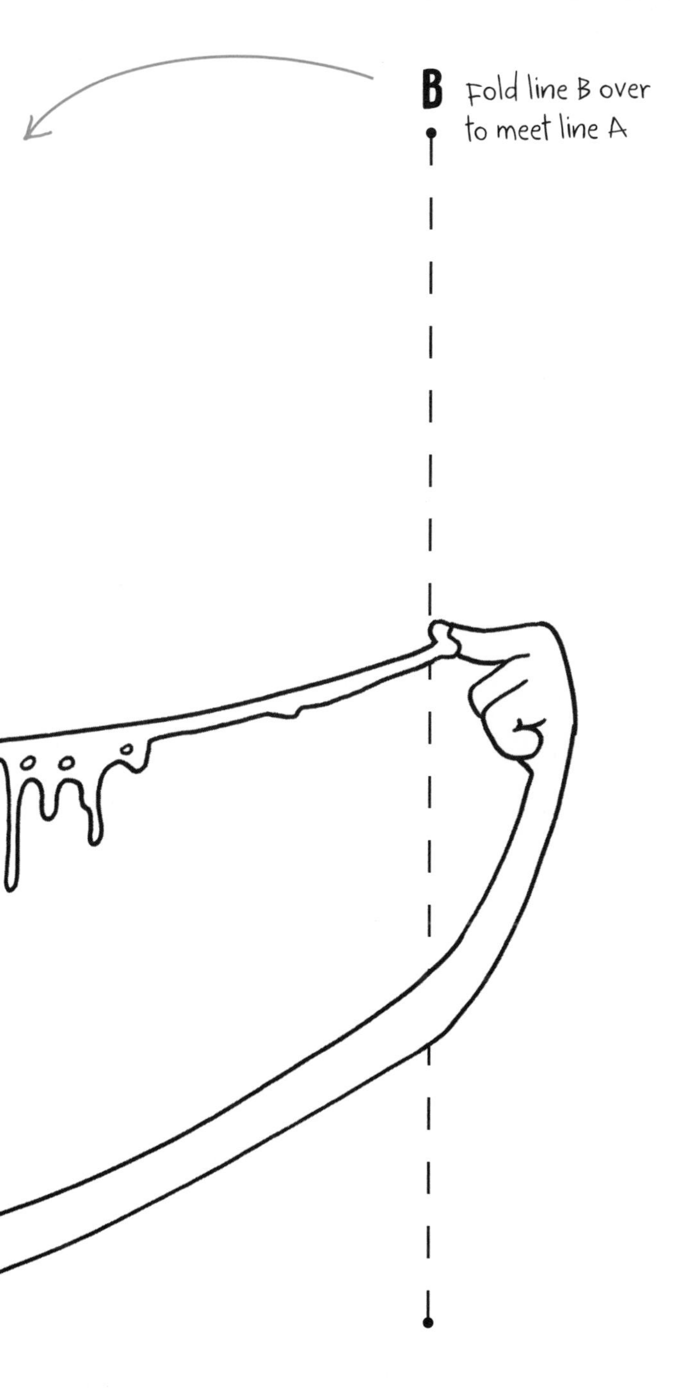

OH
NUTS!

CHAPTER 4

The day of the **soccer try-outs** came up **really** fast. Mr McDoool was going to be the coach. He set up the goals at the far end of the grass.

You might remember the name I made up for him . . .

We were all lined up, ready to show Mr McDool how well we could kick the **ball into the net**.

Henry was first.

'You're up!' said Mr McDool.

Henry kicked the ball **so high** and **so far** that we all just stood there for ages, waiting for it to come back down again!

When it landed, it rolled **right into the goal!**

Wow!

HEN-RY! HEN-RY! HEN-RY!

Bella kicked the ball **so hard** that it looked like it had been **fired** out of a **cannon** »»

and then it **slammed** into

the back of the net!

Wow!

Toby Hogan was up next. His soccer shorts showed off **even more** of his **bum** than his school shorts. It was

very

distracting.

Surely he's not going to be **THAT** *good,* I thought to myself.

'Watch this, everyone,' he said. 'I'm going to kick this into the top left corner of the net.'

Toby ran up to the ball

and

it.

HA! I thought, as it **slammed** right into the **tuckshop door**!

But then it **rebounded** onto the **bubbler** . . .

bounced on a **bin** . . .

flung off the **fence** . . .

and shot into the top left corner of the net!

Just like he said!

Wow! They were **all** so good!

Then it was **MY** turn!

I made sure my boots were tied up **extra tight**...

then I ran to the ball and **kicked**!

OH NO! It took off **diagonally** and headed straight for **James Nott**!

'Sorry!' I called out.

'That's okay,' said James, 'it knocked a

really

sticky booger

off my finger!'

Mr McDool collected the ball and dropped it at my feet. 'Just try again, Weir,' he said.

'Okay,' I said.

OH NO! This time the ball was **bounding** straight for a pair of **squirrels**!

SMASH!
OH NUTS!

Bella patted me on the shoulder. 'Don't worry, Weir,' she said. 'Just give it one more go.'

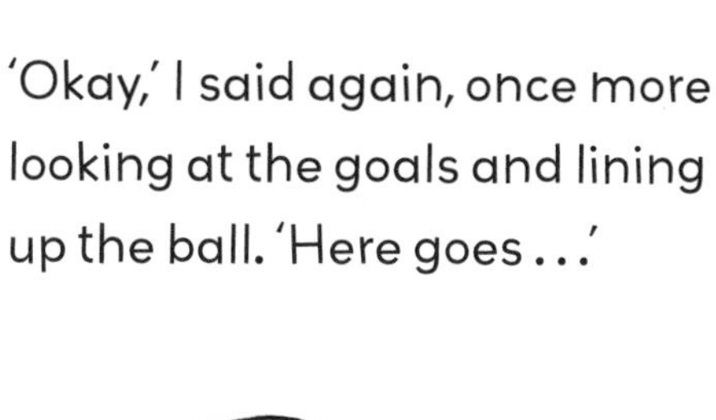

'Okay,' I said again, once more looking at the goals and lining up the ball. 'Here goes . . .'

KICK!

Uh-oh . . .

It flew straight up into a **tree**.

SQUAWK!

SPLAT!

YOU
AGAIN!

YOU
AGAIN!

I **REALLY** wanted to make the team, but my kicking wasn't going so well. **Not well at all!**

I looked at the net again . . .

I know! I'll try out for **goalie**!

I stood in the goal as Blake Green came **running towards me**, dribbling the ball. He looked like an **angry bull** that was about to **trample me!**

I ran on the spot, and **bounced** left and right, hoping I'd be able to stop the ball!

But how?!

Then **suddenly**, something **flew** in my face.

I **swatted** my hands around like **crazy**, trying to stop the **attack** . . . when all of a sudden I heard **cheering**!

Huh?

I couldn't believe it!
I'd **accidentally** swatted the ball away . . .

I'd saved the goal!

Mr McDool came up to me and shook my hand.

HANDY!

CHAPTER 5

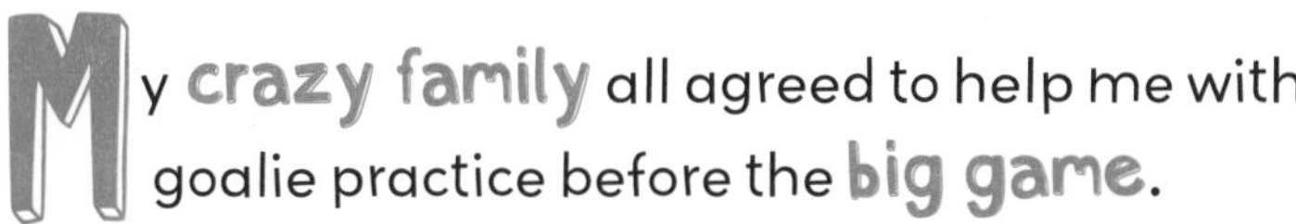

My **crazy family** all agreed to help me with goalie practice before the **big game**.

Mum set up a goal in the backyard for me . . .

. . . and everyone took turns kicking the ball.

I'm good at **a lot** of things. Drawing, building cubby houses, laughing at Henry. . . but I don't think I'm very good at

blocking

soccer

balls!

UGH!
SIGH

Time for a break!

We all went inside to help Dad with his **dancing** instead.

His routine was looking **awesome**!

Mum and I even made him a **costume**. We made a hat, a shiny vest, and a bow-tie!

Mum **loved** the costume **so much** that we ended up making one for her, too!

Dad was finally ready for the **big show**!

TWO
TUTUS!

CHAPTER 6

Dad was **super excited** about the *Talent Quest*.

We **couldn't wait** to see him dance!

The announcer stepped up on the stage and everyone in the crowd went quiet.

I HAVE A SPECIAL ANNOUNCEMENT TO MAKE . . .
ENTER AS PAIRS AND WE'LL **DOUBLE** THE PRIZE!

THAT'S RIGHT. ENTER AS PAIRS TO WIN TWO YEARS' WORTH OF DOG FOOD!

YAY! YAY! YAY!

Mum looked straight at me.

'No,' I said, '**not me!**
Roger should do it. He's **cute**!
Everyone will **love** him, even if he doesn't get the moves right!'

'My vote's for Weir,' said Dad.
'Me too,' said Sally.
'Me three,' said Granddad.

Oh yeah, did I mention
Roger can't say **Weir** yet? Every time he tries, it comes out sounding like '**Wee**'.

Mum took off her **paper plate hat** and put it on me.

The first act was Helga, the **Samples Lady** from the grocery store. Remember her?

She **sang** with her **sausage dog** and its **thirteen puppies**!

The dogs were **soooooooooo cute!**

Henry's twin brothers were up next. They had prepared a **ballet routine.**

They **spun around** all over the stage and even ended with one twin picking the other twin up!

WOW! GASP! OOOH!

Then it was our turn.

Dad decided that because we were **a pair of Dos**, our dance act should be called

THE DODOs.

I didn't think this was a great idea because:

a. Dodos aren't very good dancers

b. Dodos are extinct

Oh well . . .

I followed Dad up onto the stage. I was **REALLY nervous**, but he wasn't.

Everyone was looking at us.

The music began and I started to **sweat**.

I spotted Bella and her mum in the crowd.

Dad looked over at me and tipped his hat. I tipped mine back.

And then we **danced** ...

The crowd **laughed** and **laughed**.

HA HA HA HA HA HA

I didn't really know if they were meant to be laughing, but it didn't matter because

they LOVED us!

They **cheered so loudly** the whole time! I think they especially loved Dad's **sprinkler** and **shopping trolley**.

And they really liked our **itchy bottom squirrel**!

It was **so much fun**!

After us, there were a bunch of other **cool acts** . . . and then it was time to announce **the winners**.

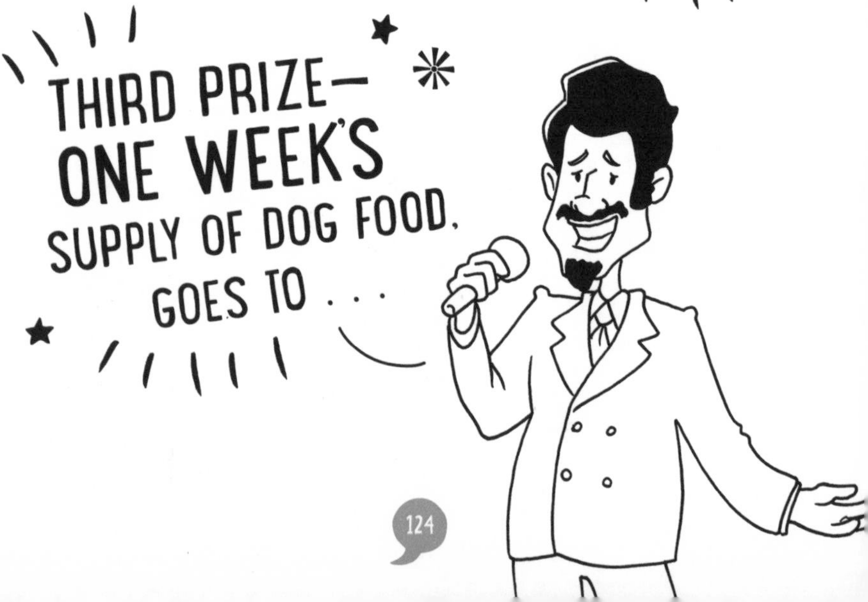

THIRD PRIZE—
ONE WEEK'S
SUPPLY OF DOG FOOD,
GOES TO . . .

SECOND PRIZE— ONE MONTH'S SUPPLY OF DOG FOOD, GOES TO . . .

AND FIRST PRIZE,
FOR THEIR UNFORGETTABLE DANCE ACT,
GOES TO . . . THE DODOS!
CONGRATULATIONS!

Dad's **great** at dancing.

And I guess I'm **not so bad** either.

It took ages filling up the car with our winnings—

TWO years' supply

of dog food!

Once it was all in there, we could barely fit!

'What are we going to do with it all?' asked Granddad, after we'd finally squeezed into the car.

'We'll think of something,' said Mum.

THE BIG GAME!

CHAPTER 7

It wasn't easy getting changed in the car! But I was **finally** ready for

the BIG GAME!

My teammates think I'm going to be great as the **goalie**!

Mr McDool too! He gave me a pair of my very own **goalie gloves**.

I really hope I do okay!

BRRRRRR!

The ref blew the whistle and the game began!

Bella and Henry were **AMAZING!**

Henry booted one of his **high** balls and it landed **right** in the net!

Then Bella kicked the ball
so hard and
so fast »»

that the other team's goalie had

NO chance

of stopping it!

We were winning 2-0!

But then their left wing player came running towards me with the ball. He ran past Clare, he ran past Toby . . . and soon it was

just me!

The boy was **real fast**!

I started stepping side to side. I didn't know what to do.

He kicked it right at me . . .

And I

ducked

it.

The ball went in. The other team had scored.

I wanted to run away and hide.

But I didn't want to let my team down.

I looked over at Dad.

He was **so proud** of me, just for giving it a go.

He was **jumping** up and down and **cheering** me on, even **throwing** in some of his **winning dance moves**.

Suddenly I had the

BEST idea **ever!**

Soon another guy came charging towards me with the ball.

I could feel the sweat **dripping** down my face.

He kicked the ball and it

»»» **shot at me like a bullet**!

But instead of ducking . . .

I did Dad's
sprinkler
dance move!
BAM!
I blocked the ball!

WOW! GREAT SAVE!

Moments later, a girl was **charging** towards me with the ball.

She dribbled left and right, then left again . . . then booted the ball to my right!

I did Dad's **snake move**.

I blocked the ball again!

WOW! ANOTHER GREAT SAVE!

We were still **one goal ahead**, with only a few minutes to go!

I just **couldn't** let one more in!

And then, in the final moments of the match, the left wing was back.

He looked more **determined** than ever to get one past me.

But I was

MORE determined

to stop him!

He **smashed** the ball at the goals, and I tried my **biggest move** ...

the killer whale!

I **leapt** out to the side and came

crashing

down on the grass.

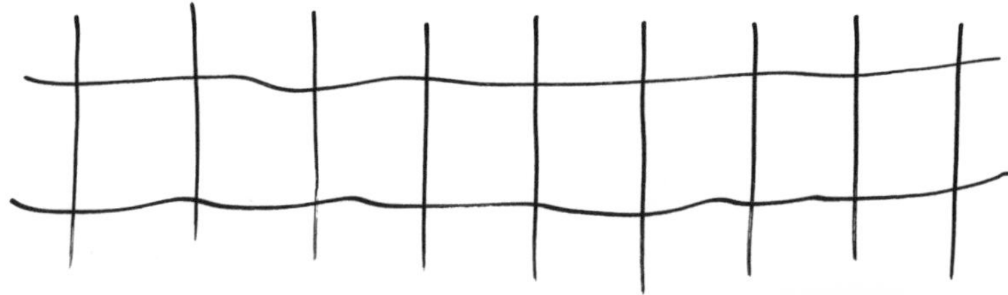

And then I looked up . . .

The ball was in my arms!

That was the whistle!

I'd never been **happier** to hear my name!

What an awesome game!
VICTORY DANCE!
break-dancing Roger

My whole family was still **celebrating** as we drove home.

Mum said there was one stop we had to make on the way.

We pulled up outside the home of Helga, the **Samples Lady** with the **singing sausage dogs**.

Mum and Dad got all the **dog food** out of the car.

Mum and Dad were inside Helga's place for a **loooooooong time**.

When they came out again, Dad was still carrying half the dog food.

And Mum was carrying something too.

Mum and Dad had

bought us a PUPPY!

What did we call him?

For the booger masters

FROM ANH

Xavier,
Luc and Leon,
who helped me
create the booger book.

ACKNOWLEDGEMENTS

FROM JULES

For Pete and Carmen and
their boys Lucas and Daniel,
who are all the
most expert of friends.

AUSTRALIAN BOOK INDUSTRY AWARDS WINNER!

Book 1

GOT IT!

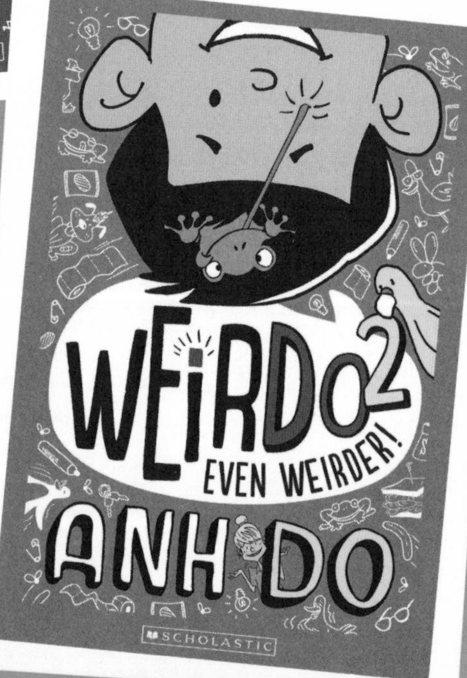

bird

Book 2

GOT IT!

COLLECT THEM ALL!

YOU CAN NEVER HAVE TOO MANY WEIRDOS

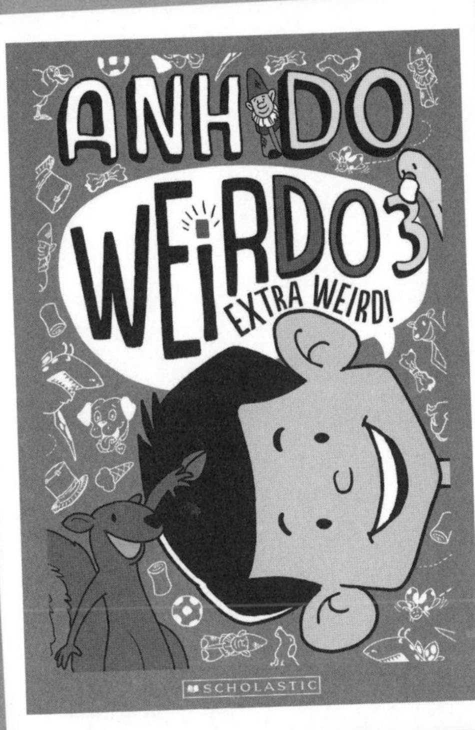

MORE
TO COME!